HALF-PIPE
PRIZE

BY JAKE MADDOX

illustrated by Tuesday Mourning

text by Eric Stevens

WITHDRAWN

STONE ARCH BOOKS

Impact Books are published by Stone Arch Books
151 Good Counsel Drive, P.O. Box 669
Mankato, Minnesota 56002
www.stonearchbooks.com

Library of Congress Cataloging-in-Publication Data

Maddox, Jake.
  Half-pipe prize / by Jake Maddox ; text by Eric Stevens ; illustrated by
Tuesday Mourning.
     p. cm. — (Impact books. A Jake Maddox sports story)
  ISBN 978-1-4342-1607-6
[1. Snowboarding—Fiction.] I. Stevens, Eric, 1974- II. Mourning,
Tuesday, ill. III. Title.
  PZ7.M25643Hal 2010
  [Fic]—dc22

                              2009004071

Summary:
When Tess moved away from Winterfall, she left her two best friends,
Ana and Sofie, behind. She's traveling back to surprise them and to take
part in the yearly snowboarding competition. Ana is glad to see her, but
Sofie acts strange as soon as Tess returns.

Creative Director: Heather Kindseth
Graphic Designer: Emily Harris

Photo Credit: Shutterstock Images/ Close Encounters Photography,
cover (background)

Printed in the United States of America

TABLE OF *CONTENTS*

Chapter 1

WINTERFALL

For the last fifty miles, I don't think I stopped smiling for even one second. That's because my mom and dad and I were driving up to Winterfall.

"How much longer?" I asked my dad.

He smiled. "Didn't you just ask me that, Tess?" he said.

"That was a long time ago," I replied. "At least ten minutes."

"We've still got a while to go," Dad said. "At least another hour."

"I hope we don't hit any traffic," my mom added.

We live down in River City, but we're not from there. To us, River City is too crowded, too busy, and too dirty. I guess that's because until this past summer, my family lived in Winterfall.

Winterfall is a tiny town. It only has one diner and one grocery store. It's pretty cold all year round. The first snow is usually in October. My dad says that's why it's called Winterfall, because winter starts in fall!

In fact, there's only one reason most people ever go to Winterfall. That reason is Grizzly Mountain, the best skiing and snowboarding mountain in the state.

Growing up in Winterfall, I learned to snowboard almost before I could walk. Snowboarding is my favorite thing in the world.

My best friends Sofie and Ana and I used to snowboard every day. After school, we'd go straight to the mountain and ride all afternoon right until dinner. Some weekends we hardly did anything other than snowboard!

The best part is we all got to ride for free. All of us had a parent working at Grizzly Mountain Resort, so our ski lift tickets were always free.

This past summer, though, both of my parents got new jobs down in River City. So we had to move. It was really hard for me to leave Winterfall.

I made my parents promise to take me back to Winterfall every winter for a week.

Now we were almost there. I couldn't wait to see my best friends and hit the slopes.

Chapter 2

REUNION

My dad pulled our station wagon into a parking space at the resort. "Finally!" I said. He had hardly stopped the car before I opened my door.

Right away, I grabbed my board and boots from the back of the car. Then I headed toward the lodge to change into my snowboarding clothes.

"Don't go too far!" my mom called out. "And be careful!"

"Meet us back at the lodge for lunch at one!" my dad added.

"Okay!" I called back with a smile.

For a moment, I glanced around the lodge, looking for Sofie and Ana. I pulled my cell phone from my pocket, but there was no signal.

I shook my head. "Stupid mountain," I said to myself. "Always blocks my signal."

After one more look around, I sat down on a bench to put my boots on. In a few minutes, I was all set.

I put my board under my arm. Then I headed toward the ski lifts.

I was sad I hadn't seen Sofie and Ana. But they didn't know I would be there. I was planning to surprise them.

Every winter, Grizzly Mountain Resort has a snowboarding competition called the GMR Cup. Anyone can enter the Cup in their age group, but one of the employees' kids always wins.

It makes sense. Kids from the city just don't get to practice nearly as much as kids who live in Winterfall.

I don't like to brag, but I won four years in a row. Sofie came in second every time.

This winter, I made sure my parents planned our week in Winterfall so I could compete again. I wanted to be the first kid from River City to win — even if I hadn't lived there very long.

I got in line for the lift to the top of the mountain. Just then, I heard my name.

"Tess?" a voice said. "Is that you?"

I turned around and saw Sofie and Ana coming out of the lodge.

"It is her!" Ana said.

Ana was smiling like crazy, but Sofie wasn't looking at me. She was looking down at the ground.

"Hi!" I called back, waving. I gave up my place in line to run over to my friends.

"I can't believe you're here," Ana said. She glanced over at Sofie.

"Hi, Tess," Sofie said. She tried to smile, but I could tell she wasn't really happy. She still wouldn't look me in the eye.

"Hi, you two," I replied.

My good mood was starting to fade. To be honest, I was expecting a happier reunion than this.

"I'm here for the whole week," I went on. "That means I can compete in the Cup!"

Ana looked at Sofie again. "That's great, Tess," Sofie said. "Really."

Then she turned around and went back into the lodge without saying another word.

Chapter 3

LEFT OUT

"What was that all about?" I asked Ana.

"I'm not sure," Ana replied. She tried to smile. "I'll go and check on her."

Ana quickly chased after Sofie. I picked up my board and tried to keep up. By the time I got through a small crowd and into the lodge, I couldn't see them anywhere.

I sat down on a bench near the door and looked at a nearby clock.

It was already 11:30. I didn't have much time before lunch with my parents.

After a few minutes, Sofie and Ana walked over. I stood up.

"Is everything okay?" I asked. It was weird to feel so out of touch with my friends. Something was obviously going on, but they didn't want to tell me about it.

"Yes," Sofie said. "I just had to, um, go to the bathroom."

"Well, should we go for a few runs?" I asked.

"For sure," Ana replied. She smiled at me, and I smiled back. At least Ana seemed happy I was back in Winterfall.

Soon we were on the three-person lift up to the top of Grizzly Mountain. I felt the cold mountain wind blow across my face.

The air got even colder as we glided higher and higher up the mountain.

"I have missed this so much," I said, smiling.

"You've only been away for like five months," Sofie said. "It's not like you've been gone for five years or something like that."

I didn't know what to say to that, so I looked at my hands. "I just missed it," I said quietly.

The ride to the top of Grizzly Mountain is pretty long. But when your best friend is giving you the cold shoulder, it feels like it takes about a million years to get to the top.

Finally, I saw the peak. "Here it comes," Ana said.

I turned and smiled at her. I was glad she sat between Sofie and me on the lift. It would have been even harder otherwise.

As the lift reached the drop-off spot, I stood up and let my board take me off the lift. The three of us glided a few feet. Then we stopped in a place where we wouldn't get in the way of other skiers or boarders.

From the top of the mountain, you can choose a few different routes. Some are fast and steep, and others are a little slower.

"Which way should we go?" I asked.

Sofie shrugged. "Doesn't matter," she said without looking at me.

Ana looked at Sofie, then at me. She smiled and said, "Yeah, you should choose, Tess. You've been away, after all."

"Okay," I said.

I looked up at the trails sign. I wasn't sure which one to choose.

"She can't even remember the different choices," Sofie said. I frowned. She was acting like I couldn't even hear her.

"You know, I'm standing right here," I said.

"Whatever," Sofie said. "Just pick a trail so we don't freeze to death."

I stared at Sofie. She didn't look back. I felt myself starting to get very upset. Instead of getting into a fight with Sofie, I just picked a trail.

Without a word, I pushed off and glided to the top of Maple Run. I clipped my back foot into the board and started down. I didn't even care if Sofie and Ana were behind me or not.

Chapter 4

QUICK RUN

I had a good run, but it wasn't as fun as I'd hoped it would be. I wasn't even thinking about snowboarding. Instead, I was too busy feeling sad about Sofie.

I had no idea why she was so mad at me. I hadn't seen her since July. I couldn't have done anything wrong.

When I reached the bottom, I turned to look for my friends. They weren't in line for the lift.

After a few minutes watching people reach the bottom of the run, I still didn't spot my two friends. I kept looking for a while, but I didn't see them anywhere.

The big clock over the lift line said 12:30. I was supposed to meet my parents in half an hour.

I guess I have time for one more run, I thought.

I got back in the lift line. Soon I was soaring over the trees on my way back to the peak.

About halfway up the mountain, I spotted Ana and Sofie below me. They were on Hairpins and Needles, one of my favorite trails.

They took a different trail, I thought. *Probably so they could talk about me.*

When I reached the top, I realized I only had about ten minutes before I was supposed to meet my parents at the lodge. They hated it when I was late for things.

"Guess I better take Straight Shooter," I said to myself. That trail was the quickest way down.

Soon I was flying down the slope. It's pretty much a straight line from the top to the bottom.

Of course, you can't just go straight down the whole way. Your speed would be way too high!

Instead, you have to cut back and forth the whole time. But you still go pretty fast.

I got to the bottom in good time. When I stopped, a spray of snow shot out in front of my board.

Even though my friends were being weird, I couldn't help smiling and feeling good. I was back in Winterfall on my board!

I quickly took off my board and ran into the lodge. It was 12:55.

"And I even have five minutes to spare," I said to myself. Then I spotted Ana and Sofie eating lunch.

I walked over to my friends. Right away, I turned to Sofie. It was time to get to the bottom of this.

"Hi, Sofie," I said.

She didn't reply. She just kept looking down.

"Look," I went on, "obviously you're mad at me about something."

"No," Ana said. "She's not. Don't worry, Tess."

Just then, my parents walked over to us.

"Hi, sweetie," my mom said. "Hi, girls."

Ana said hello, but Sofie just sat there. Now she was just being plain rude. "Hello, Sofie?" I said.

Finally she turned and looked at me. "Just go back to River City, Tess," she shouted. "Okay?" Then Sofie got to her feet and stormed off.

Chapter 5

LUNCH

My favorite food in the entire world is the macaroni and cheese at Grizzly Mountain Resort's café. But that day, I barely touched it. I just poked at it with my fork and leaned on my fist.

"You're pretty mad at Sofie, huh?" my dad said.

I just shrugged.

"Try not to let her ruin this week for you, sweetie," my mom added.

"I won't," I said. "I don't even care, really."

"You don't, huh?" my dad asked.

"No, I don't," I replied. "I only wanted to come up so I could compete in the Cup anyway."

"Hmm," my mom said. "If I remember right, you haven't even mentioned the Cup."

"That's right," my dad added. "You only talked about Ana and Sofie for the last month, since we started planning this trip."

Maybe that was true, but I didn't care anymore. For the rest of the week, I planned to just snowboard and think about the Cup.

My appetite started coming back. The mac and cheese was as great as ever.

"Remember, honey," Dad finally said after a few minutes of silent eating. "Sofie was your best friend for years."

"I know," I said. "So what?"

"So," Mom replied. My parents always talk as a team like that. They like to finish each other's sentences. "So maybe she's a little angry at you for leaving Winterfall."

"It wasn't my choice to leave!" I replied. "That's dumb."

"Maybe," Dad said. "But sometimes people get upset over dumb things."

I looked down at my food. I wasn't hungry anymore.

Chapter 6

SITTING OUT

Sometimes, I'm happy when I'm right and my parents are wrong. This time, I wasn't happy.

The next morning, I found Sofie and Ana at breakfast.

The café has a great buffet breakfast. Piles of fresh fruit, eggs any way you want them, and all kinds of yummy sausage and bacon and stuff. It's a great breakfast before a long day on the slopes.

"Hi, Ana," I said. I joined them in line for the buffet. "Hi, Sofie," I added quickly.

"Good morning, Tess," Ana replied. Sofie, of course, didn't say anything.

"Sofie," I went on, "I know why you're mad at me."

She spun and faced me. "Oh, do you?" she asked. "Why am I mad at you?"

"Because I moved to River City," I said. "But I didn't want to move. I would rather have stayed in Winterfall with you two forever."

Sofie just glared at me. Then she dropped her tray and stomped off toward the bathroom.

"I guess my parents were wrong," I said to Ana. "They said she was hurt because I moved away."

"Nah," Ana said. "We know you had to move because of your parents' new jobs."

"Then what is it, Ana?" I said. I felt desperate. "Why is Sofie so mad at me?"

Ana glanced at the bathroom door to make sure Sofie wasn't coming back. She wasn't, so Ana turned toward me. "You know how you win the Cup every year?" Ana asked.

I nodded. "Of course," I replied.

"And Sofie always came in second every year?" Ana asked.

Again, I nodded. "Yes," I said.

"Well," Ana went on, "when you left, of course we knew we would miss you. But Sofie also realized she had a great chance of winning the Cup this year."

Then I realized what was going on. "So, with me here this week," I said, "Sofie thinks I'll win again."

Ana nodded. "She pretty much thinks you came back this week just so she couldn't win," Ana said.

"That's crazy!" I said. "I would never do that!"

"I know you didn't do it on purpose," Ana said. "But Sofie isn't so sure."

That's when Sofie walked over. "Are you talking about me?" she asked.

"Yes," I said. "Sofie, I didn't come back to take the Cup from you."

Sofie looked at me. Her eyes were soft, like she'd been crying. "You didn't?" she asked.

"Of course not," I said. "I thought it would be fun to be in the Cup with you two again, that's all."

"Well, it will be, I guess," Sofie replied.

No one said anything. We were probably really holding up the line for the buffet.

"Listen," I said finally, "I won't even enter the Cup."

"What?" Ana said.

"You won't?" Sofie asked.

I shook my head and reached for the bacon. "Nope," I replied. "I'm going to sit this one out and cheer for my friends Sofie and Ana."

I moved down the line and filled my plate. The next thing I knew, Sofie threw her arms around my neck.

"Thank you, Tess!" Sofie said. "I really appreciate it."

Well, we were friends again. We ate breakfast together and spent the rest of the day making run after run on our snowboards.

I watched my friends as they shot down the slopes. Sofie had really gotten better with her jumps and tricks. She even pulled off a perfect 360.

It was nice that no one was angry at anyone else. But by the end of the day, I felt sort of empty inside.

The truth is, I really wanted to enter the Cup.

Chapter 7

SIGN UP

After a few days, I was starting to feel pretty sad. I mean, I was happy to see my friends again. I was especially happy that Sofie wasn't angry at me anymore. That had been the worst feeling.

But it seemed like we had just switched places. Sofie was having a great time now. She was smiling all the time and having a lot of fun on the slopes. It was nice to see her so happy.

Meanwhile, I was hardly trying at all on my snowboard. My tricks were lame, my speed was slow, and I wasn't really having fun.

Early on Friday morning, the day before the competition, we headed over to the half-pipe. That's a long ditch on the slope for doing tricks.

Ana and I sat on the edge. We watched Sofie take a run through the pipe.

"Sofie has been practicing on the pipe a lot, huh?" I asked. I could tell from her tricks that she'd been working hard. She was landing much better than she used to. She seemed much more confident.

"Constantly," Ana replied with a nod. "She spends all afternoon on the pipe, after school is out."

"What about you?" I asked.

Ana shrugged. "I prefer the downhill, I guess," she said. "It's cool."

We watched Sofie take one last trick off the lip. It was a perfect 360 with a front grab. I was impressed.

Sofie stuck the landing perfectly and then slid out the bottom of the pipe. Ana and I coasted down to meet her.

"That was great, Sofie," I said. "You've gotten so much better at the half-pipe!"

"Thanks," she replied. Then she looked at the big clock over the chair lift. "We better get to the lodge," Sofie said, turning to Ana. "We need to get our names on the list for the Cup."

"Oh, yeah!" Ana said. "Sign-up starts at ten this morning."

The two of them turned and glided toward the lodge. I watched them for a minute.

"I can't believe I'm not going to be in the Cup," I muttered to myself. Then I turned and followed my friends to the lodge.

By the time I got to the lodge and took off my board and helmet, my friends were standing in front of the sign-up list. I walked up and stood behind them.

"There," Sofie said, putting down the pen. "I'm ready for the Cup."

Ana picked up the pen and scrawled her name on the sign-up list. "Me too," Ana said.

Sofie nodded. "This will be my year!" she said happily.

Then Sofie turned and saw me standing behind her. She took a breath and sighed. "Tess," Sofie said. "This is dumb."

"What is?" I asked. For some reason, I couldn't look her in the eye.

Sofie laughed. "You know what," she said. I felt her arm around my shoulder.

"I was being a big baby," Sofie went on. Then she said to Ana, "Give me that pen."

Ana glanced at me, and I shrugged. She picked up the pen and handed it to Sofie.

"Thank you," Sofie said. Then she scribbled something on the sign-up list. "There."

"What did you do?" I asked. I looked over her shoulder. She had written my name on the sign-up list!

"Sofie!" I said. "But I promised not to be in the Cup this year."

"I know," Sofie replied. She picked up her helmet and snowboard. "But like I said, that was dumb."

I smiled at her. "Thanks, Sofie," I said. "And to be honest, you're so good on that half-pipe now, I'm pretty worried about my chances anyway."

Sofie laughed. "Then we better get out there and practice," she said. "You don't want to embarrass yourself."

Chapter 8

DOWNHILL RACE

The Cup began on Saturday morning. The bottom of the slope was covered in different colored flags to show where the different groups should gather. My group's flag was yellow and had a big "11 to 13" on it.

There were ten girls competing in our group. Of course, we knew most of the other girls. They had all been at Grizzly Mountain since we were little.

There were a few girls we didn't know. We figured they were probably from River City. I wondered if someday I'd know them better than I know Sofie and Ana.

A woman walked up to our flag. I recognized her from the last season.

"Hi, girls," she said. "I'm Angie, and I'm in charge of your group for the Cup."

"Hi, Angie," we all replied at once. A few of us giggled.

Angie leaned toward me. "I'm glad to see you here, Tess," she said. "Can't have the Cup without our champ!"

I smiled. "Thanks, Angie," I said.

"Okay, so as most of you know," Angie said, "the Cup is two events. A downhill race, and the half-pipe."

Angie looked at the clock. "We'll be doing the downhill first, in about ten minutes," she said. "So get loosened up, get your gear on, and get in line for the lift."

Ana raised her hand. "What trail are we running?" she asked. "I mean, for the race part."

"Hairpins and Needles this year," Angie replied. "Should be a good race!"

Soon, the ten of us, and Angie, were at the top of the mountain.

We were all set to start the race. We were lined up on a thick black line that had been painted right on the snow.

"Remember, the girl in first gets five points," Angie went on. "Second place gets four points, and third place gets three points."

"What about the pipe?" asked one of the girls I didn't know.

"The pipe will be scored by the judges," Angie said. "The highest possible score is five. So the total score to aim for is ten."

"What did you get when you won last year?" a girl asked me.

I know I blushed then. "Um, I got 8.8," I said.

"Tess is the best on the mountain," Sofie said, throwing her arm around me.

I shook my head. "Not this year," I said.

"Okay, girls," Angie said. "Let's do this!"

We all cheered.

"Ready," Angie announced, "set . . . go!"

We all shot off the starting line.

Hairpins and Needles is one of the trickiest trails on Grizzly Mountain. It's full of really sharp turns and sudden steep drops. I love it.

Around the first curve, Ana, Sofie, and I were really close. At one point, we could have reached out and grabbed each other's hands. We reached the first jump at the same time and launched together.

"Woo!" Ana called out. Sofie and I laughed.

"We're totally winning!" Sofie called out. I could hardly hear her over the rushing air and the sound of our boards on the snow.

It was a great run. But before long, we reached the top of the last steep drop. The finish line was at the bottom. I could see a small crowd gathered around.

I leaned and cut sharp into the snow. I'm usually faster on these downhill races than Sofie and Ana.

I glanced over my shoulder. Sofie was close behind me, and Ana was close behind her. I saw a few other girls coming over the last lip, not far behind Ana.

In a split second, I was across the finish line. With my arms in the air, I cut sharply to stop, sending a spray of fluffy snow in front of me. Sofie and Ana finished right after I did.

A voice crackled over the slope loudspeaker. "In the girls 11 to 13 group," the voice said, "the winner is last year's Cup champ, Tess Harris, with five points!"

Sofie and Ana were at my side. They each gave me a high five.

"In second with four points, Sofie Waller," the voice went on, "and that's three points to Ana Moore for third place."

"Good job, Tess," Sofie said. "But watch your back on that half-pipe!" she added with a smile.

"Oh, I will," I replied.

The truth was, I didn't even care about winning. For the first time since I came back to Winterfall, we were all happy.

Chapter 9

THE PIPE

We took a break for lunch (with lots of cocoa). Then the girls from our group met with Angie at the top of the half-pipe.

"Here's the fun part, girls," Angie announced. "Time to really show off."

"Who are the judges?" a girl asked.

Angie pointed at a long table near the bottom of the pipe. There were four people sitting at the table.

"Those are the judges," Angie said. "They are the head of the patrol, the head of the ski school, the winner of last year's adult Cup, and the owner of the resort."

Sofie whistled. "Wow," she said.

"Yeah, they're a good group of skiers and snowboarders," Angie said. "They definitely know their stuff. So do your best out there!"

With that, Angie called out the first to hit the half-pipe. It wasn't anyone we knew well.

The girl dropped into the pipe and started her routine. She didn't fall or anything, but none of her tricks were hard.

"Boring," Sofie whispered to me and Ana. "You have to try tougher tricks than those."

The judges took a few moments, then showed her score: 2.5. Not bad, but not good enough to win.

Ana went next. She must have really listened to Sofie. She went for a 360 on her very first trick.

She made it, but almost fell. Sofie and I cheered like crazy.

"Good job, Ana!" I called out.

After her turn, the judges held up a 3.1. We went crazy cheering.

"She beat her score from last year," I pointed out.

Next it was my turn. I hopped over to the top of the pipe.

"Whenever you're ready," Angie said with smile.

I pulled on my goggles and clipped into my board. Then, with a nod to Angie, I dropped in.

Right away, I pulled off a smooth grab with a lot of air. The landing was perfect.

On the next trick, I decided to go for a 360. But I wobbled on the landing, just like Ana had.

I guess I was a little out of practice from being in River City. After all, there's not a mountain there that I can practice on every day.

To end my run, I pulled off a couple of clean 180s and then glided out the bottom of the half-pipe.

After cutting into a stop, I turned to face the judges and pulled off my goggles and helmet. I knew I'd done okay, but not great.

The judges lifted my score card: 3.3. That wasn't as good as last year's score.

Still, it was pretty good. To beat me, Sofie would have to score better than a 4.3. I was pretty sure she could do it.

A few more girls took their turns. Sofie went last on the pipe. The highest score in our group had been 3.5. That meant Sofie's turn in the pipe would have to be pretty amazing.

From the bottom, Ana and I watched her drop in. She hit the first trick with a lot of speed.

"Wow," I said. "She wasn't even doing her best the other day, huh?"

Ana shook her head. "Nah," she said. "That was just for fun. She's really amazing on the pipe now."

And she was. Sofie's first trick was a 360 front grab. She stuck it perfectly. Everyone cheered like mad.

She did trick after trick. She didn't wobble. She looked confident. She just kept impressing us.

Once, she got so much air she was able to grab the back of her board and pull it up almost to her helmet. It was amazing.

When Sofie came out of the pipe, it sounded like the whole resort was cheering for her. I know Ana and I sure were!

It only took about a second for the judges to hold up their score card. Sofie got a 4.9!

"Sofie!" I called out, running over to her. I threw my arms around her neck. "That was amazing!"

She hugged me back. "Thanks, Tess," Sofie said, smiling. "But I'm just glad you were here to be with me."

I smiled back. "Me too," I said.

A voice crackled over the loudspeaker. "With a record score of 4.9 on the pipe, and a total score of 8.9 for the competition," the voice said, "the winner for the girls 11 to 13 group is Sofie Waller!"

Angie came running over. She was carrying the trophy.

It was the same one I got to hold up for the last few years. But not this year.

"Congratulations, Sofie," Angie said. "I've been watching you on the pipe this season. You really deserved to win." She handed Sofie the trophy. Then she walked away.

"You really did deserve to win," I told Sofie. "Even with me in the Cup too."

"Thanks for making sure I figured that out," Sofie replied.

Sofie took my hand and held the trophy up. The crowd cheered. It felt like they were cheering for me too.

ABOUT THE AUTHOR

Eric Stevens lives in St. Paul, Minnesota. He is studying to become a middle-school English teacher. Some of his favorite things include pizza, playing video games, watching cooking shows on TV, riding his bike, and trying new restaurants. Some of his least favorite things include olives and shoveling snow.

ABOUT THE ILLUSTRATOR

When Tuesday Mourning was a little girl, she knew she wanted to be an artist when she grew up. Now, she is an illustrator who lives in Knoxville, Tennessee. She especially loves illustrating books for kids and teenagers. When she isn't illustrating, Tuesday loves spending time with her husband, who is an actor, and their son, Atticus.

GLOSSARY

compete (kuhm-PEET)—try to win

confident (KON-fuh-duhnt)—having a strong belief in your own abilities

embarrass (em-BA-ruhss)—make someone feel awkward and uncomfortable

half-pipe (HAF PIPE)—a U-shaped ramp with a flat section in the middle

lift (LIFT)—a device that carries skiers or snowboarders up a mountain

lodge (LOJ)—at a ski resort, a place to warm up

recognize (REK-ugh-nize)—to know who someone is

resort (ri-ZORT)—a place where people go for rest and relaxation

reunion (ree-YOON-yuhn)—a meeting between people who haven't seen each other for a long time

MORE ABOUT SNOWBOARDING GEAR

Want to get started snowboarding? Here's what you need.

* **A BOARD.** Check out ski and surf shops in your area. If you're looking for something cheaper, try searching online or in your local newspaper for a used board — you might find a great board for less cash.

* **FOOTWEAR.** You will need special snowboarding boots. They can be expensive, so a good pair of boots is another thing to look for in secondhand stores. You'll want a high-quality pair to keep your toes warm and safely secured to your board!

* **GOGGLES.** Going fast down snowy slopes can make the icy wind really dry out your eyes — goggles will help keep them moist, and keep the snow out of them.

* **BINDINGS.** These keep your boots strapped to your board. Buy them wherever you buy your boots.

* **OUTDOOR CLOTHING.** You're going to be snowboarding in lots of snow — you'll need to stay warm! You will want to be wearing ski pants. You'll also want a snowboarding jacket, which is longer than a traditional ski coat. To make sure you're comfortable, wear lots of layers under your outerwear.

* **A HELMET.** This isn't necessarily required, but you'll feel more comfortable knowing your noggin is safe.

* **GLOVES.** Snowboard shops sell them, but you can buy gloves anywhere — as long as they're waterproof.

Not ready to buy? You can rent most of these things at the snowboarding hill.

DISCUSSION QUESTIONS

1. Why was Sofie upset when Tess returned to Winterfall? What else could Tess have done to find out what was wrong?

2. What are some good ways to cope when you or a friend move away? How can you stay in touch while you're apart?

3. At the end of this book, Sofie wins. What do you think would have happened if Tess had won? How would the story be different?

WRITING PROMPTS

1. Try writing chapter 3 from Sofie's point of view. What does she think and feel? What does she hear and see?

2. Pretend you're Tess. Write a letter to Sofie and Ana after you leave Winterfall and return home to River City after the GMR Cup.

3. What do you think happens after this book ends? Write another chapter of this book that picks up where this book leaves off. What happens next?

SPORTS STORIES
FOR EVERY ATHLETE

BY JAKE MADDOX

Ballet Bullies

FIELD HOCKEY FIRSTS

HOOP DOCTOR

SKATER'S SECRET

SOCCER SPIRIT

STOLEN BASES

Back on the Beam

OVER NET

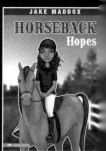

HORSEBACK Hopes

WAIT!
DON'T close the book!
There's
MORE!
FIND MORE:
Games
Puzzles
Heroes
Villains
Authors
Illustrators at...
www.
capstonekids
.com
Still want MORE?
Find cool websites and more books like this
one at www.Facthound.com.
Just type in the Book ID: 9781434216076
and you're ready to go!